cloverleaf books™

Where I Live

This Is My Neighborhood

Lisa Bullard

illustrated by Holli Conger

M MILLBROOK PRESS · MINNEAPOLIS

For Wendy, my favorite neighbor

Millbrook Press
A division of Lerner Publishing Group, Inc.
241 First Avenue North
Minneapolis, MN 55401 USA

For reading levels and more information, look up this title at
www.lernerbooks.com.

Main body text set in Slappy Inline 18/28.
Typeface provided by T26.

Library of Congress Cataloging-in-Publication Data

Names: Bullard, Lisa, author. | Conger, Holli, illustrator.
Title: This is my neighborhood / Lisa Bullard ; illustrated by Holli
    Conger.
Description: Minneapolis : Millbrook Press, [2016] | Series: Cloverleaf
    books : where I live | Includes bibliographical references and
    index.
Identifiers: LCCN 2015035269 | ISBN 9781467795210
    (lb : alk. paper) | ISBN 9781467797375 (pb : alk. paper) |
    ISBN 9781467797382 (eb pdf : alk. paper)
Subjects: LCSH: Neighborliness—Juvenile literature. | Neighbors—
    Juvenile literature. | Neighborhoods—Juvenile literature.
Classification: LCC BJ1533.N4 B85 2016 | DDC 177/.1—dc23

LC record available at http://lccn.loc.gov/2015035269

Manufactured in the United States of America
1 – BP – 7/15/16

TABLE OF CONTENTS

Chapter One

A Neighbor Needs Help

"Malik!" called my new neighbor. "Buddy's run away, and I'm so worried! Can you help me find him?"

A neighborhood is a group of people and buildings in one area. Neighborhoods are sometimes called communities.

"Sure, Mrs. Z.," I said. "I know this neighborhood better than anybody! I'll tell Dad where I'm going. Then I'll meet you out front."

Dad and I met Mrs. Z. on the sidewalk. "Why do you think Buddy ran?" I asked.

"We used to live on a farm in the country," she said.

"There was a lot of open space to run.
Buddy forgets he lives in a neighborhood now."

Neighborhoods in the city have many buildings and houses. Rural neighborhoods in the country have fewer buildings and people.

"The park has lots of open space," I said. "Let's start there!" Dad said he could help. We hurried in that direction, calling Buddy's name.

Chapter Two

Searching the Neighborhood

My best friend lives in an apartment by the park. I ran up the steps and rang the buzzer. "Elena, can you help us find Buddy?"

Apartment buildings have different homes and families under one roof. Some city neighborhoods have many apartment buildings.

Mr. Roberts was waiting at the bus stop and heard us calling Buddy. "A dog was barking over there." He pointed up the hill at the school. "I'll help you search. My shopping can wait!"

"We'll cover more ground if we split up," Mr. Roberts said. He and Mrs. Z. headed uphill. The rest of us kept going toward the park. We passed a lemonade stand. The kids there hadn't seen Buddy.

My babysitter Olivia was at the park playing
basketball. We asked if she'd seen a black-
and-white dog running loose. "I haven't," she
said, "but why don't you climb to the top of
the slide? You'll be able to see farther."

We didn't see Buddy, but we did see a worker high up in a bucket truck. She shook her head at our question. "Sorry, kids. I haven't seen him, and when I'm up there, I can see all the way from Johnson Street to Park Street."

MARIO'S PIZZA

BUS STOP

LEWISVILLE POWER CO.

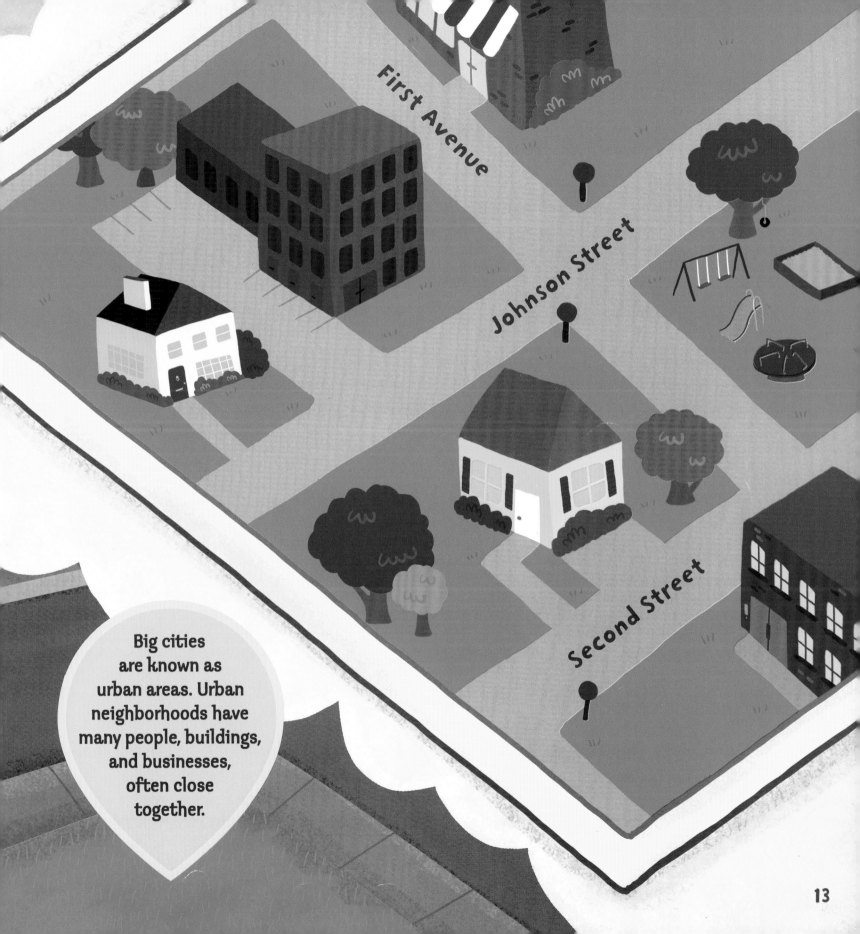

First Avenue

Johnson Street

Second Street

Big cities are known as urban areas. Urban neighborhoods have many people, buildings, and businesses, often close together.

13

Chapter Three

A New Idea

"Maybe we should hang a Lost Dog sign somewhere," I said.
"Good idea!" Dad answered. "We can walk over to the coffee shop and leave one there."

Neighborhoods just outside of bigger cities are called suburbs. These neighborhoods often have many homes but few businesses.

15

"We'd better go home and get paper
and markers to make a sign," I said.

We headed down a different block, still calling for Buddy. We met Mrs. Z. and Mr. Roberts. I told them about our idea for a sign.

"I've got the perfect photo of Buddy we can add," said Mrs. Z.

Chapter Four

Surprise!

Elena and I hurried around the corner onto our street.
And there was Buddy—sound asleep on Mrs. Z.'s front step!

"Buddy's here!" I called to the others. "He's safe!"

Mrs. Z. told Dad we deserved a reward for helping, even though Buddy really found himself! We walked to the coffee shop with Buddy on his leash.

FREE LIBRARY

"Thanks, Mrs. Z.," I said and took a big bite of my treat. "I didn't really need a reward. Dad says helping out is the neighborly thing to do. But this cupcake tastes pretty neighborly too!"

What is your neighborhood like? Are the houses and shops close together, or are they farther apart?

21

Try it: Neighborhood Map Hunt

Malik and his friends looked all over the neighborhood for Buddy. Can you find these places on the map of their neighborhood below? Can you find these same places in the story's pictures too?

- Mrs. Z.'s house
- Malik's house
- Elena's apartment
- the bus stop
- the park
- the coffee shop

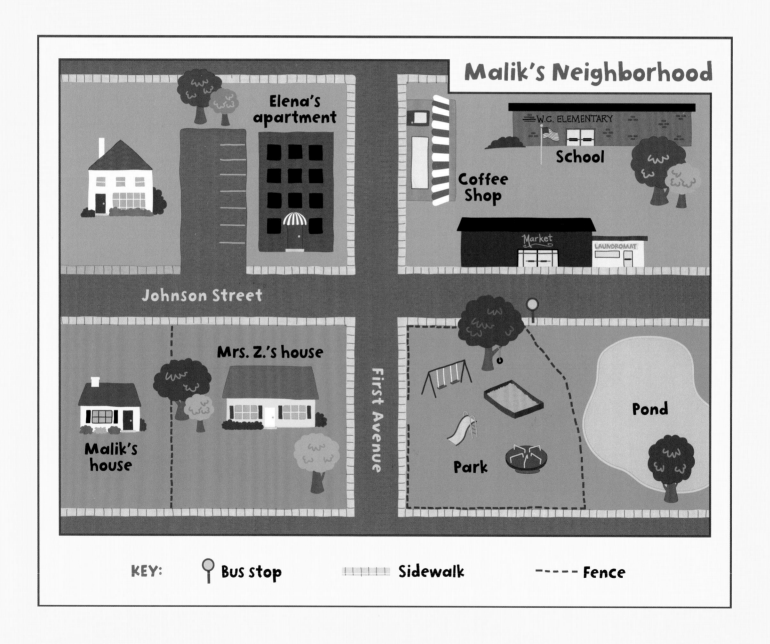

GLOSSARY

apartment: a home inside a larger building

bucket truck: a vehicle that can lift workers in a bucket up high

community: a group of people who have something in common

neighborhood: a group of people and buildings together in an area

neighborly: helpful and friendly to those who live nearby

rural: far from big cities with fewer people and buildings

suburb: an area just outside of a big city

urban: in or near a big city

BOOKS

Boothroyd, Jennifer. *Map My Neighborhood*. Minneapolis: Lerner Publications, 2014. Learn how to make a map of the neighborhood where you live.

Brown, Tameka Fryer. *Around Our Way on Neighbors' Day*. New York: Abrams, 2010. Join the fun as one city neighborhood celebrates Neighbors' Day.

McDonald, Caryl. *Rural Life, Urban Life*. New York: Rosen, 2014. Learn more about how rural and urban neighborhoods are alike and different.

WEBSITES

Brain POP Jr.
https://jr.brainpop.com/socialstudies/communities/ruralsuburbanandurban/draganddrop
Play a matching game to decide which things go with a rural neighborhood and which things go with an urban neighborhood.

PBS Kids: Build a Neighborhood
http://pbskids.org/rogers/buildANeighborhood.html#hold
Click and drag the pictures on this website to build your own neighborhood.

Types of Communities
http://www.eduplace.com/kids/socsci/books/applications/imaps/maps/g3_u1/
Explore a map showing differences between urban, suburban, and rural neighborhoods.

LERNER SOURCE
Expand learning beyond the printed book. Download free, complementary educational resources for this book from our website, www.lernersource.com.